SHOO FLY!

SHOO FLY!

As told and illustrated by

Iza Trapani

📖 Charlesbridge

Published by Charlesbridge
85 Main Street
Watertown, MA 02472
(617) 926-0329
www.charlesbridge.com

Library of Congress Cataloging-in-Publication Data

Trapani, Iza.
Shoo fly / Iza Trapani.
p. cm.
Summary: In this illustrated version of a familiar song, a mouse tries to get rid
of a pesky, unwanted playmate.
ISBN 978-1-58089-052-6 (reinforced for library use)
ISBN 978-1-58089-076-2 (softcover)
ISBN 978-1-60734-198-7 (ebook)
1. Children's songs—United States—Texts. [1. Mice—Songs and music.
2. Flies—Songs and music. 3. Songs.] I. Title.
PZ8.3.T686 Sh 2000
782.42164'0268—dc21
[E]   00-024592

Printed in Korea
(hc) 10 9 8 7 6 5 4 3 2 1
(sc) 10 9 8 7 6 5 4 3 2

Illustrations done in watercolors on Arches 300 lb. cold press watercolor paper
Display type and text type set in Freestyle Script Bold and Tiffany Medium
Printed October 2012 by Sung In Printing in Gunpo-Si, Kyonggi-Do, Korea
Book production by *The Kids at Our House*
Designed by *The Kids at Our House*

*For Eric and Tasha,
with love*

Shoo fly don't bother me,
Shoo fly don't bother me,
Shoo fly don't bother me—
I belong to somebody.

That fly has gone away—
At last I'm free to play.
I told that pest to scram—
Now I'm happy as a clam.

Shoo fly don't bother me!
You're not my cup of tea.
Please stop annoying me—
Kindly go and let me be.

I think I'll find a nook,
Curl up and read a book.
Some nice and quiet spot—
Someplace where that fly is not.

Shoo fly don't bother me!
Go fly to Tennessee.
Leave on the count of three—
Can't you see you're bugging me?

I need to go outside
And find a place to hide.
My plan had better work,
Or I'll really go berserk.

Shoo fly don't bother me!
Please leave immediately.
Fly far away from me—
I don't want your company.

My tummy has a hunch
That it could use some lunch.
I think the coast is clear—
No more buzzing in my ear.

Shoo fly don't bother me!
Go find your family.
Go hide up in a tree.
Just don't stay and pester me!

I really need a rest
From that unwelcome guest.
I'd better take a nap;
Otherwise I think I'll snap.

Shoo fly don't bother me!
Go spread your wings and flee
Across the great blue sea,
All the way to Waikiki.

I'm beat without a doubt—
That fly has worn me out!
So now I'll close my eyes—
Hope that I don't dream of flies.

Shoo fly don't bother me,
Shoo fly don't bother me,
Shoo fly don't bother me—
I belong to somebody.

SHOO FLY!

Shoo fly don't both - er me, Shoo fly don't
both - er me, Shoo fly don't both - er me—
I be - long to some - bod - y.

2. That fly has gone away—
   At last I'm free to play.
   I told that pest to scram—
   Now I'm happy as a clam.

3. Shoo fly don't bother me!
   You're not my cup of tea.
   Please stop annoying me—
   Kindly go and let me be.

4. I think I'll find a nook,
   Curl up and read a book.
   Some nice and quiet spot—
   Someplace where that fly is not.

5. Shoo fly don't bother me!
   Go fly to Tennessee.
   Leave on the count of three—
   Can't you see you're bugging me?

6. I need to go outside
   And find a place to hide.
   My plan had better work,
   Or I'll really go berserk.

7. Shoo fly don't bother me!
   Please leave immediately.
   Fly far away from me—
   I don't want your company.

8. My tummy has a hunch
   That it could use some lunch.
   I think the coast is clear—
   No more buzzing in my ear.

9. Shoo fly don't bother me!
   Go find your family.
   Go hide up in a tree.
   Just don't stay and pester me!

10. I really need a rest
    From that unwelcome guest.
    I'd better take a nap;
    Otherwise I think I'll snap.

11. Shoo fly don't bother me!
    Go spread your wings and flee
    Across the great blue sea,
    All the way to Waikiki.

12. I'm beat without a doubt—
    That fly has worn me out!
    So now I'll close my eyes—
    Hope that I don't dream of flies.

13. Shoo fly don't bother me,
    Shoo fly don't bother me,
    Shoo fly don't bother me—
    I belong to somebody.